Royse C. Roberts has been married to her husband, Archie, for 35 years. Being a blended family, she has four daughters, six grandchildren, and eight great-grandchildren. She has previously written a book titled *Mr. & Mrs. Wren,* in which she named the Wrens' baby chicks by some of her great-grandchildren. She wrote for her own pleasure, had a friend illustrate the story, and presented the book to her great-grandchildren on Christmas 2017. During the spring of 2018, she believed God was directing her to write a story about her oldest great-grandson, who developed type 1 diabetes at the age of seven. Thus, the story of *Let's Pretend* was born.

ROYSE C. ROBERTS

AUSTIN MACAULEY PUBLISHERS™

LONDON ★ CAMBRIDGE ★ NEW YORK ★ SHARJAH

Copyright © Royse C. Roberts (2020)

Ordering Information:
Quantity sales: special discounts are available on quantity purchases by corporations, associations, and others. For details, contact the publisher at the address below.

Publisher's Cataloging-in-Publication data
Roberts, Royse C.
Let's Pretend

ISBN 9781645751847 (Paperback)
ISBN 9781645751830 (Hardback)
ISBN 9781645751854 (ePub e-book)

Library of Congress Control Number: 2020903843

www.austinmacauley.com/us

First Published (2020)
Austin Macauley Publishers LLC
40 Wall Street, 28th Floor
New York, NY 10005
USA
mail-usa@austinmacauley.com
+1 (646) 5125767

To my great-grandson, Pierson Hall, and his inspiration to children everywhere.

I am grateful to my husband Archie and two of my friends, Jane Posey and Phyllis Sanford, who encouraged me after I had written the story of *Let's Pretend* about my great-grandson, Pierson, to take a step of faith and pursue the possibility of having the story published. They have been my faithful cheerleaders throughout the process.

My name is Pierson,
I am ten years old.
I have a story that has not been told,
I would like to tell it,
If I could be so bold!

When I was 7, not 8 or 9,
my life changed
but I am fine.
I developed childhood diabetes,
it would change my life completely.

Changes had to be made in my daily life,
especially my way of thinking.
I needed to manage the issues involved,
so that some problems could be resolved.

6

Mom, Dad, T. P. and Posh
have helped me a lot, oh my gosh!
The seminars and training of every kind
have brought to me peace of mind.

And three years later, just look at me,
I am almost fit as any kid could be!

8

I play soccer, flag football, and like to swim,
I will grow to be healthy, tall, and trim.

If I am ever feeling blue,
which is something I seldom do,
I close my eyes really tight
and make a wish with all my might.

I make a plan to play PRETEND.
If you want to join me in this game,
just close your eyes and let's begin
our game of LET'S PRETEND.

LET'S
PRETEND

We can pretend to fly up to the sky
and show other kids how to fly,
with our new wings we can try.

If flying is not what you want to do,
we can march to the zoo.
The zoo has animals of every kind,
let's see if a monkey we can find!

Then, guess what else we can pretend to do?
Be like a monkey in the zoo,
we swing around the cage,
until a new pretend we have made...

12

What about a circus act?
Well, we could do it, that's a fact.

Why not pretend to be a clown
and paint our face on upside down?

Or, the flying trapeze appeals to me,
swinging high above the ground.
The audience would yell and clap their hands,
no better trapeze artist could be found.

18

Another pretend we could possibly be,
an astronaut, so we could see
the Earth from way up in the sky,
riding our spaceship as we fly.

20

Would you like to be a cowpoke?
Let's join the rodeo.
We could ride a bucking horse,
hold on tight, holler, and scream,
until we have no voice.

22

What about a racecar driver
speeding around the track?
We could set our goals to win that race,
finishing in first place, never looking back.

24

Or we could pretend to be a fireman
and rescue kids who call for help.
Here we come, just wait and see,
all you kids can count on me.

26

The policeman wants to be our friend,
can we pretend to be one of them?
He protects us from all kinds of crime,
Sure, we can do it, just give us time!

28

To be a scientist would be the best pretend,
we would be on a mission over and over again.
Finding the perfect treatment for kids everywhere,
to be free of illness, they would have a story to share.

Victory! Victory over illness would be our goal.
Kids would be able to laugh, dance, and play,
if only in PRETEND, we could make their day.

CPSIA information can be obtained
at www.ICGtesting.com
Printed in the USA
LVHW070454280620
659170LV00003B/75